A, B, C

My e Sound Box

by Jane Belk Moncure
illustrated by Vera Gohman

THE CHILD'S WORLD

MANKATO, MN 56001

Library of Congress Cataloging in Publication Data

Moncure, Jane Belk.
  My "e" sound box.

  (Sound box books)
  Summary: The eggs and elves in Little e's sound box
have a bumpy ride on an elephant.
  1. Children's stories, American.   [1. Alphabet]
I. Gohman, Vera Kennedy, 1922-   ill.   II. Title.
III. Series.
PZ7.M739Mye   1984   [E]   84-17021
ISBN 0-89565-297-8 -1991 Edition

My "e" Sound Box

(This book concentrates on the short "e" sound in the story line. Words beginning with the long "e" sound are included at the end of the book.)

Little  had a box.

"I will find things that begin with my 'e' sound," he said.

"I will put them into my sound  box."

Little found eggs,

lots and lots of eggs.

Did he put the eggs
into his box?

He did.

Then Little  found elves.

The elves danced and danced.

Did Little  put the elves into the box with the eggs?

He did.

The elves played with the eggs.

"Be careful, elves," said Little .

Now the box was heavy.

So Little  found an elephant,

a big elephant.

"Hop on," said the elephant.

The elephant went up and down. . . .

The eggs fell out of the box.

The elves fell too.

So did Little

"That was a bad bump," he said.

"What a mess," said Little e.

"Now who will help me fill my box?"

An Eskimo  came by.

"I will help you
fill your box,"
said the Eskimo.

box

"I know where we can find
lots of eggs," said the Eskimo.

Guess who had eggs,
eggs, eggs for Little ?

box

Guess who had pretty eggs for everyone?

elephant

box

elves

eggs

Eskimo

27

Can you read these words with Little 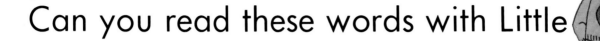?

elevator

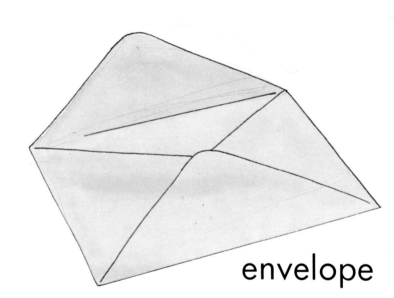

envelope

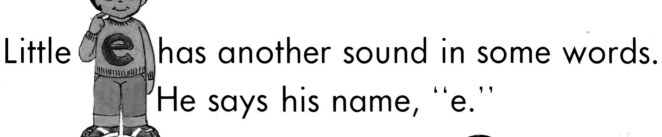

Little e has another sound in some words.

He says his name, "e."

Can you read these words?

Listen for Little e 's name.

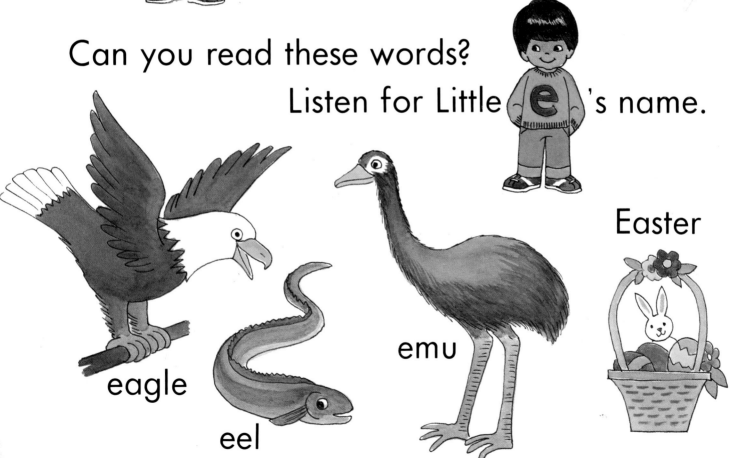

eagle

eel

emu

Easter

29

About the Author

Jane Belk Moncure began her writing career when she was in kindergarten. She has never stopped writing. Many of her children's stories and poems have been published, to the delight of young readers, including her son Jim, whose childhood experiences found their way into many of her books.

Mrs. Moncure's writing is based upon an active career in early childhood education. A recipient of an M.A. degree from Columbia University, Mrs. Moncure has taught and directed nursery, kindergarten, and primary grade programs in California, New York, Virginia, and North Carolina. As a member of the faculties of Virginia Commonwealth University and the University of Richmond, she taught prospective teachers in early childhood education.

Mrs. Moncure has traveled extensively abroad, studying early childhood programs in the United Kingdom, The Netherlands, and Switzerland. She was the first president of the Virginia Association for Early Childhood Education and received its award for oustanding service to young children.

A resident of North Carolina, Mrs. Moncure is currently a full-time writer and educational consultant. She is married to Dr. James A. Moncure, former vice president of Elon College.